# Annie and the
# Wild Animals

# Annie
## and the
# Wild Animals

Written and Illustrated by
### JAN BRETT

Houghton Mifflin Company

Boston

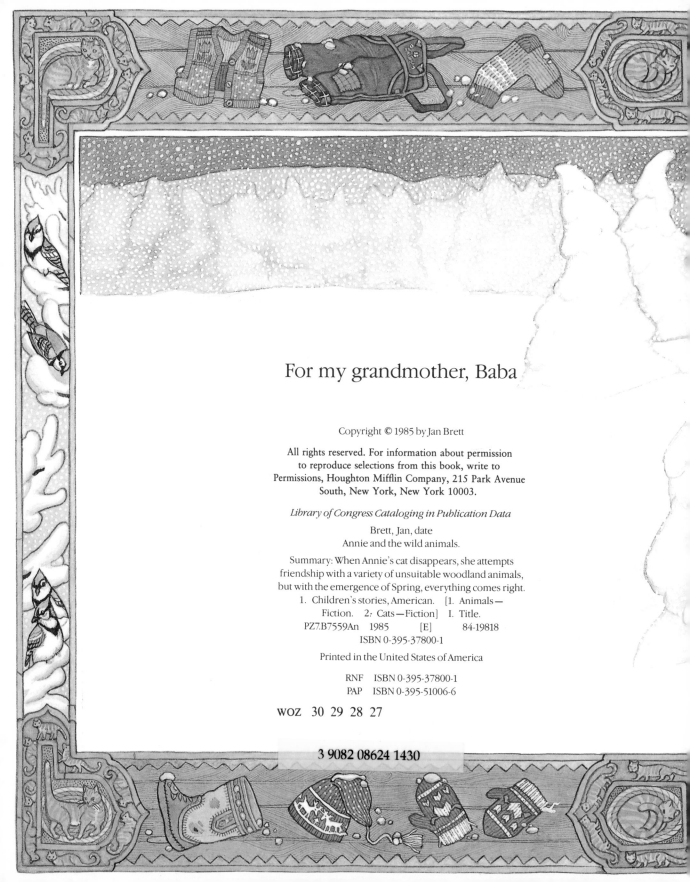

For my grandmother, Baba

Copyright © 1985 by Jan Brett

*Library of Congress Cataloging in Publication Data*

Brett, Jan, date
Annie and the wild animals.

Summary: When Annie's cat disappears, she attempts
friendship with a variety of unsuitable woodland animals,
but with the emergence of Spring, everything comes right.
1. Children's stories, American.   [1. Animals —
Fiction.   2. Cats — Fiction]   I. Title.
PZ7.B7559An  1985      [E]       84-19818
ISBN 0-395-37800-1

Printed in the United States of America

RNF   ISBN 0-395-37800-1
PAP   ISBN 0-395-51006-6

WOZ   30  29  28  27

It had been snowing for days.
Winter was lasting too long.

Something was wrong with Annie's cat.
Taffy had stopped playing.

She ate more than usual.

She slept all day long.

Annie found her curled up in strange places.

One morning Annie could not find Taffy anywhere.
She looked and looked, but Taffy was gone.
Annie was very lonely.

"I need a new friend," thought Annie.

She placed a corn cake at the edge of the wood.
She imagined that a small, furry animal would
come and she would tame him for a pet.

The next morning the corn cake was gone.
In its place stood a giant moose.

"He's too big to tame," thought Annie.
"I'll have to try again."
That night Annie left another corn cake
at the edge of the wood.

The next morning the moose was back and
a snarling wildcat was there too.
"He's too mean to tame," thought Annie.

Annie placed more corn cakes at the edge of the wood.

The next morning a big, growling bear was there
with the moose and the wildcat.

"He's too grumpy for a pet," thought Annie.

Annie made as many corn cakes as she could
and left them at the edge of the wood.

At dawn Annie heard the snarls and growls
of the wild animals.
There was the moose—and the wildcat
and the bear.

They had been joined by a stag, his family,
and a large, gray wolf.
"Not one of them is soft and friendly like Taffy,"
thought Annie.

All the next day Annie made corn cakes and
left them at the edge of the wood.
All night long she heard the sounds of the
wild animals eating the corn cakes.

Annie awoke to find a great nose stuck
through her window.
It belonged to the moose,
who was still hungry.

There were wild animals everywhere.
They roared for their next meal.
The little house shook.

The animals wanted more corn cakes.
But when Annie looked into the barrel of corn meal,
It was empty.
She couldn't make any more corn cakes.

Annie was very sad. She would never find
a pet now.
She missed Taffy very much.

All that night a warm breeze blew from the south.
The snow melted and new buds could be seen
on the plants and trees. The wood was coming
alive again.
By the next morning the wild animals had gone
back to the wood. They would find
food there, now that spring had finally come.

Then, as unexpected as the warm spring breeze,
Taffy walked proudly into the yard.

"Taffy," Annie exclaimed, "you have come home.
Where have you been?"
Taffy turned and looked back the way
she had come.

Out of the wood came three soft and
friendly kittens.
Annie would not be lonely anymore.